To every child who was laughed at, picked on, or thought they'd never be anything, think again. The world is what you make it. You don't have to fit in, you just have to be tough enough to stand out!
Dr. Roo

For all the little Brodys out there; may you be the best that you can be.
Kimberly G

For families who are looking for hope in their lives.
Miss. Alex

Brody The Lion was created by Dr. Kristin Wegner, PhD, LP, illustrated by Alexandra Garcia, with additional assistance by Kimberly Sattler, MS/BCBA.
Published by Autism and Behavior Center, Altoona, WI. © 2020 All rights reserved.
The art in this book is all digitally created. Typesets used in this book are Zubilo, SS Farmhouse Lemonade Regular, and Playtime with Hot Toddies.

# SOMETIMES I ROAR!

## Written by Dr. Kristin Wegner
## Illustrated by Alexandra Garcia
### Parent and Therapy Pages Co-Authored by
### Kimberly Sattler, Ms/BCBA

Brody the Lion was as proud as could be,
his birthday was coming, he was going to be 3.
He wanted a party, with cake and balloons,
all of his friends and lots of good tunes.

He wrote out the cards, please be here at 9:00,
there's lots of fun planned, so please be on time.
He sent one to Snake, Hippo, and Bear,
and Monkey of course, she would be there.

When party day came,
Brody was ready.
He waited for Monkey,
Snake, Hip, and Teddy.

But 9:00 came, and no friends in sight.

Brody roared a big roar,

NO! THIS NOT RIGHT!

Then Brody sat
to wait patiently,
until he saw Hip,
Snake, Bear, and Monkey.

His friends all had presents, with ribbons and bows.

They gave them to Brody,
who jumped on his toes.

Brody opened Snake's present;
a castle and knight.

Brody roared a big roar,

NO! THIS IS NOT RIGHT!

I know you were hoping for a new train;
but things can be different,
they don't have to be same.
Dad said Brody, you know what to do;
take a **deep breath**, and **count to 2**.

Brody took a
and blew a

Deep Breath
Big Blow

he smiled to Snake and said thank you.

The time had come for cake and ice cream.
"**Hurray for Brody**", friends started to scream.
As his friends sang, Brody covered his ears.
Then came the **roar**, and
down came the **tears**.

Mama said Brody you know what to do;
take a **deep breath**, and **count to 2**.

Brody took a

Deep Breath

and blew a

Big Blow

he said, ok Mom, I'm ready to go.

His friends kept on singing;
Brody put down his paw.
He blew out his candles,
then came the applause.

Brody wanted to cover his ears and shout "**NO!**"

**BUT**

Brody took a Deep Breath and blew a Big Blow

When the cake was eaten, game time began.
Brody was ready, he had a good plan.
But Hippo and Monkey wanted to dance,

Bear and Snake said, **we'll take a chance!**

Brody roared a big roar,

NO! THIS IS NOT RIGHT!

I don't want to dance, not now, not tonight!

Dad said Brody you know what to do;
take a deep breath, and count to 2.

he said, ok Dad, I'm ready to go.

Dad started the music and Brody joined in.
Monkey said loudly,

**let's see who can win!**

The music kept playing and then it would stop.
The winner would be the first one to drop.

Monkey was first to fall to the floor.
Brody could feel the start of a roar.

Mama said Brody you know what to do;
take a **deep breath**, and **count to 2**.

Brody took a

Deep Breath

and blew a

Big Blow

he said, ok Mom, I'm ready to go.

The friends kept on dancing,
and having good fun;
until Mom said, it's time to be done.

Brody felt the roar growing loud,
but he took a breath and made Mama proud.

His friends said goodnight, Brody headed to bed;
Mom pulled the covers and patted his head.
You're a good little Lion, have a good night;
just remember, things don't have to be right.

# READ THE STORY TO MATCH CHILD'S NEEDS

## See examples at www.BrodytheLion.com

❋ **For Children who do not speak or use Single Words:**

Do not read the text as written. Use 2-3 words that the child understands for each page.

❋ **Children who use 2-4 words:**

Read some of the text and focus on what the characters are doing and feeling. Read the text that repeats "No that is not Right" or "Brody you know what to do".

❋ **Children who speak in Full Sentences:**

Read the book as written.

## HELP CHILDREN READ THE STORY WITH YOU.

❋ **Turning pages:**

Even the youngest child or child with complex needs can help turn pages.

❋ **Filling in the repetitive text:**

There are repeating lines from the story that children can anticipate. Create a pattern by using dramatic voice tones, facial expressions, and gestures (stomping feet).

❋ **Identifying pictures:**

Have children point to pictures in the book. Ask children to find smaller pictures in the scene or label actions of the characters.

❋ **Ask Questions:**

Examples: Who is coming to Brody's party? What did Snake give Brody? What do you think Brody will do? What would you do? What could Brody have done differently

# THERAPEUTIC TIPS

The challenges Brody faces in the story are recognizable by those who love a child with special needs including autism. Brody roared when his friends were late, he didn't get the present he wanted, singing was too loud, his game plan changed, and he lost dance dance drop. Many children become frustrated when faced with unexpected events like these. For most children, however, frustration doesn't lead to a meltdown. This is because they manage their emotions by regulating their behavior. Behavioral regulation occurs in the prefrontal cortex which is the executive functioning part of the brain. When a child is having a meltdown, the part of the brain that is activated is the amygdala which is responsible for this 'fight or flight' response. Once this 'fight or flight' response has been triggered, it is not easy to help a child calm down. Trying to use behavioral regulation techniques during a meltdown is often not be effective because children will not be able to take a breath and blow if they have not already learned this skill.

If your child experiences meltdowns, especially if your child exhibits dangerous or aggressive behaviors, consult a licensed behavior analyst, a clinical psychologist, or social worker trained in Applied Behavior Analysis (ABA) to develop a behavior plan. Behavior Plans outline what to do during a meltdown. Behavior plans also outline strategies to prevent meltdowns include avoiding triggers, giving warnings, creating social stories, and using predictive schedules. These are excellent techniques and can help avoid meltdowns. In addition to responding to meltdowns and using strategies to prevent meltdowns, behavior plans outline how to teach replacement behaviors for identified triggers. For example, if your child has a meltdown because of a loud sound, you can teach your child to tolerate unexpected sounds. In the story, Brody's parents were able to coach Brody to take a deep breath and count to 2. This worked for Brody because Brody had already learned and practiced the behavioral regulation steps outlined below.

## TEACHING BEHAVIORAL REGULATION

🍀 The first step is to teach behavioral regulation when there is no trigger. Practice taking a breath and calming when your child is happy, calm, and relaxed. Make sure there are no other demands. Visit www.brodythelion.com for examples.

🍀 After your child can take a deep breath when calm, practice with a slightly accelerated heart rate. This is still practice WITHOUT a trigger. Start playing an activity your child enjoys that accelerates heart rate but does not overstimulate. This may include chasing, ticking, dancing, etc. Pause the activity, take a breath, and when your child is calm, continue the activity. Do not res ume play until your child has calmed. The length of pause varies on how long it takes your child to calm.

🍀 If your child becomes upset when activities like chasing, tickling, or dancing are paused; before practicing breathing, you need to teach your child to tolerate the pausing of the activity. Try dancing and pausing for a fraction of a second; resuming so quickly that there's not even enough time for your child's brain to register that it was paused. You might need to give a warning that you are going to stop the music so stopping doesn't trigger a meltdown. Celebrate successes and remember this will take time.

# HOW TO TEACH TO TOLERATE UNEXPECTED EVENTS

After your child learns to regulate their behavior with and without an accelerated heart rate, it is time to practice with triggers. A trigger is something that causes a meltdown. Think about how you react when you are going to get a shot. The sight of a needle may cause you to panic. This fight or flight response is normal. For a child with autism, the world is filled with 'needles' that elicit a panic response. Since we don't want meltdown after meltdown, and we can't eliminate all the 'needles' in your child's world; we need to teach them how to tolerate triggers. We can't give examples for every trigger, so we will focus on unexpected sounds.

Birthday Parties are noisy events. People sing, balloons pop, and there are a lot of other unexpected sounds. In the story, Brody covers his ears when his friends start singing. Children like Brody may cover their ears when the blender is turned on, they hear the vacuum, or even see the vacuum. Since these things can trigger a meltdown, we don't want to use them to practice. Remember that while you are teaching your child to tolerate noises, you should try to prevent meltdowns by avoiding items that cause meltdowns, giving a warning, or wearing headphones.

Start by picking a noise maker that you can control and that does not trigger a meltdown. A confetti popper is a good noise maker to use because most children have not seen a confetti popper before so there is not a learned association. This means they won't panic when they see a confetti popper. In addition, the falling confetti is fun to watch. Below are the steps to teach your child to tolerate loud noises using a confetti popper. Remember the confetti popper is just an example.

- Pair the confetti popper (or an item that makes a loud noise) with something positive. Do this by cheering and celebrating while showing the confetti popper.
- Practice watching the confetti popper being used without the noise. You can take a video and show to your child with the sound turned off.
- Practice watching the confetti popper with increasing volume. You can do this by increase the volume on video or watching from a different room.
- Practice shooting off the confetti popper from across the room with a warning.
- Practice shooting off the confetti popper with a time delay warning.
- Shoot the confetti popper without any warning.
- Keep practicing when not expected, different times of day, and new places.

After you have practiced with the confetti popper, move on to other noise makers like whistles, noisy toys, fog horns, etc. Start with those that do not cause meltdowns and then move to items that cause your child to react. Go slow, be patient, and don't give up! This process takes a LOT of time and a LOT of Practice. Remember that every child is unique, and every situation is different. You will need to individualize the steps to meet the needs of your child. If something you try doesn't work at first, don't give up. Do what Brody does in his next book, sing the can-do chant:

"I can do it, yes I can; I can do it, Brody can!"